Illustrated by Hallie Gillett

How Did Bible Heroes Pray?

For Evelyn,
Enjoy!
Mona Hodgson

Mona Hodgson

KREGEL
Kidzone

Where Kids are number One

How Did Bible Heroes Pray?

Text © 2004 by Mona Hodgson
Illustrations © 2004 by Hallie Gillett

Published by Kregel Kidzone, an imprint of Kregel Publications, P.O. Box 2607,
Grand Rapids, MI 49501.

Art Direction / Interior Design: John M. Lucas

ISBN 0-8254-2778-9

Printed in China

With special thanks to all who have
contributed to my life through prayer
and to all who continue to do so.

Note to Adults

Children possess an insatiable curiosity. One thing they often wonder about
is prayer. Did the men and women of the Bible kneel to pray? Did
they only pray at night? Did they pray outside?

By showing the prayer practices of some of our most-loved
Bible heroes, this book will help children develop their
own prayer lives. They will learn that they can pray anytime and anywhere. The poem at the back of the book will
reinforce this truth.

—Mona

Did you know that when you talk to God you are praying?

Have you ever wondered how Bible heroes like Daniel
and Esther prayed? I have.
What I found out is really great!

Daniel talked to God down on his knees, three times a day.
(Daniel 6:10)

You can talk to God
down on your knees, too.

Samuel prayed when he lay in his bed,
waiting and listening for God.

(1 Samuel 3:1–10)

You can pray when you lie in your bed, too.

A man who wrote psalms looked
up at the sky when he
stopped to pray.
(Psalm 123:1)

You can look up at the sky
when you talk to God, too.

Jesus, God's Son, left His disciples so He could pray by Himself.

(Luke 22:41)

You can talk to God when you
are by yourself, too.

**Hannah stood and prayed to
the Lord silently in her heart.**

(1 Samuel 1:9–13)

You can pray to God silently
in your heart, too.

Jonah was swallowed by a big fish
and talked to God about his trouble.

(Jonah 2:1–2)

You can pray when you are
in trouble, too.

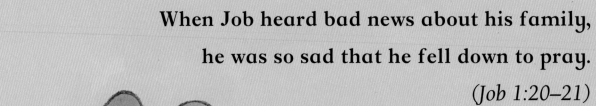

When Job heard bad news about his family,
he was so sad that he fell down to pray.

(Job 1:20–21)

You can talk to God when you are sad, too.

Queen Esther was afraid, so she prayed for three days and nights for God's help.

(Esther 4:16)

You can talk to God

when you are afraid, too.

David thanked God with joy
in his happy heart.

(2 Samuel 7:18)

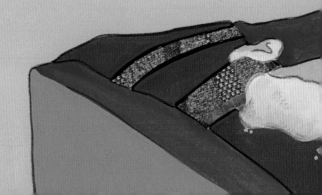

You can pray when you are happy, too.

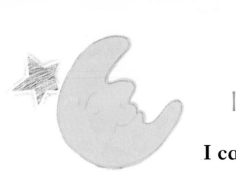

I Can Pray

I can pray when the moon glows at night.

I can pray when the sun shines bright.

I can pray lying in my bed.

I can pray standing on my head.

I can pray when I'm sad.

I can pray when I'm glad.

No matter where I am, God can hear me when I pray.

God can hear me talk to Him, anytime—night or day.